The Witch House
and other
Tales Our Settlers Told

The Witch House
and other
Tales Our Settlers Told

by JOSEPH and EDITH RASKIN

illustrated by
WILLIAM SAUTS BOCK

SCHOLASTIC BOOK SERVICES
NEW YORK • TORONTO • LONDON • AUCKLAND • SYDNEY • TOKYO

To our sister Sara

12 11 10 9 8 7 6 5 4 3 2 1 10 7 8 9/7 0 1 2/8

Printed in the U.S.A. 06

Contents

Foreword	7
The Witch House	9
The Baker's Dozen	11
A Token of Friendship	18
The Oak That Helped Outwit a King	27
Jonathan Moulton and the Devil	36
The Great Scare	46
Old Meg, the Witch	55
The Goose From Flatbush	64
A Happening on Christmas Eve	72
The Part-time Prisoner	81
Chief of the Night Riders	90
The Mystery of Pelham House	101
The White Deer of Onota	110
Kayutah, the Drop Star	120

Foreword

In colonial America, life was both difficult and challenging. Not only did people fear real dangers such as attacks by the French and Indians and the tyranny of the English kings, but they also had a superstitious dread of the supernatural. Like their fears, the tales they told in taverns and at home gatherings were a weaving of fact and fancy.

While devils, demons, and evildoers spiced some of the tales our settlers told, many stories centered about heroic generals, friendly Indian chiefs, or simply honest neighbors. As time went by, the colonial people with their romantic imaginings fashioned legends from these oft-repeated anecdotes. Those tales that have come down to us give a fascinating glimpse into the thinking, behavior, and pattern of life of the people as well as the great events of that time. Here are some of our favorites.

— Joseph and Edith Raskin

The Witch House

The stories our ancestors spun about witches, magic, and ghosts were more than an entertainment; many people sincerely believed them. There were numerous natural and everyday occurrences which they could not explain in those days. Therefore, whenever mischief or misfortune befell them, how simple it was to place the blame on the devil or an eccentric neighbor! Fortunately, there were some skeptical souls who would not accept the accusation of witchcraft against anyone based only on hearsay or rumor.

Still standing today as evidence of such a skeptical attitude is a charming old house in Pigeon Cove, Massachusetts, known merely as "the witch house." It was more than two hundred and fifty years ago that it first came by its name. When the witchcraft madness gripped the people of Salem, Massachusetts, Miss Wheeler, a lovely young woman, had the finger of suspicion pointed at her. Despairing of her life, her two brothers placed her in a boat when night fell and, rowing around Cape Ann, brought her to a house hidden in the woods of Pigeon Cove. The good people of Rockport, a settlement just two miles away, scoffed at the idea that this lovely girl was a witch. They protected her and never revealed to outsiders the whereabouts of the accused girl and her brothers.

The Baker's Dozen

Once Albany, the capital of New York State, was only a little town. There were few streets, and most of its quaint houses with tall chimneys were only one story high. It even had a different name — Beverswyck.

In that little town lived a baker whose full name was Volckert Jan Pietersen Van Amsterdam. Because his name was too big a mouthful, people just called him Baas (Master). Nobody in the whole Hudson River region baked better cookies than Baas. Not only did they taste delicious, but they were even delicious to look at, their shapes were so unusual.

During the week before the New Year, Baas always baked special cookies. These he shaped to resemble Santa Claus, then called Saint Nicholas. People took the trouble to come from faraway places to buy them.

The day before the New Year, Baas worked very hard. All day long he kept busily refilling the trays with freshly baked cookies. He could barely keep up with the people waiting to buy them. He was glad when evening came and he could lock his bakery. At last he could get into his comfortable chair before a warming fire, rest his feet, and count up all the money he had made.

As he was about to shut the door, an old woman pushed herself into the bakery. She wore a tall, battered bonnet, and all he could see of her face was a crooked nose and a long, curving chin.

"I want a dozen." The old woman pointed a

bony finger at the Saint Nicholas cookies.

Baas counted up twelve cookies, wrapped them in a paper, and gave them to her.

"One more cooky. I want a dozen!" the woman cried in a shrill voice.

"You needn't shout so loud — I am not deaf!" Baas retorted. "I gave you twelve. That's a dozen."

"One more cooky. One more than twelve makes a dozen," the woman insisted.

Baas was losing his patience. "Who put that crazy idea into your head? Twelve makes a dozen, everybody knows that!"

"One more cooky! I want a dozen," the old woman repeated.

Now Baas's patience was at an end. "If you want another cooky, go to the Devil to get it!" he snapped. Then, grabbing the old woman by the shoulder, he pushed her out of the bakery.

The old woman went away. But from that time on, strange things began to happen in Baas's bakery. One day Baas baked a trayful of cookies. They looked so good that he was proud to put them on the counter. Almost immediately a customer came in and wanted to buy some. Baas started to reach for them, but suddenly the cookies and the tray were not there — they just disappeared! Another time Baas put some loaves of bread into the oven. Right before his eyes the loaves rose so high and became so light that they flew up the chimney. The next day Baas again tried to bake bread. When he opened the door of the oven, the loaves of bread turned over on their sides and rolled out like hoops. They hit him on the chest, knocking him over. One morning he baked a new batch of cookies. This time again the cookies looked as fine as ever. But at the very moment he was taking them out of the oven, one oven brick fell, then another. Before he could step back, one brick knocked the cookies right out of his hand.

No matter how hard he tried, he had practically no cookies or bread to sell. Fewer and fewer people came to his bakery.

Things went from bad to worse. His wife became ill, then his children became sick. By the time the New Year holiday came, Baas was completely discouraged.

Standing alone in his bakery, he pleaded aloud, "Dear Saint Nicholas, advise me what to do."

Before he finished saying it, the kindly Saint Nicholas appeared before him. "What can I do for you?" he asked, smiling.

"Please advise me," Baas begged.

"Well, Baas," Saint Nicholas said, "you are a good baker. But you must learn to be generous to people. Next time that old woman comes, give her what she asks."

"I promise," Baas vowed.

Saint Nicholas disappeared as suddenly as he had appeared. Just as suddenly, the old woman stood in his place.

"I want a dozen cookies," she demanded.

Readily Baas counted thirteen cookies, almost all he had been able to bake, and gave them to her. "A happy New Year to you," he said politely.

The old woman counted the cookies. "The spell is broken!" she exclaimed. "No more will misfortune visit you."

Telling Baas to lay his hand on a Saint Nicholas cooky, she made him swear that he would be generous in the future.

She started to leave, then stopped and shook her finger at the baker. "Remember this day," she said. "From now on a dozen is thirteen. It shall be known as a baker's dozen!"

So it was. As long as the colonies lasted, giving extra measure was commonly practiced. However, when the thirteen new states declared their independence and formed the United States of America, the smart Yankees restored the original measure of a dozen. But the custom of giving a baker's dozen has lingered on to this day.

A Token of Friendship

Back in the colonial days in the northern part of New York State there lived an Oneida tribe of Indians whose chief was Han Yerry. To this land came Judge White with some settlers to found the town of Whitesborough. At first the Indians were not happy to have the palefaces as their neighbors. How could they be trusted? They took land that belonged to the Indians, and they killed off so many wild animals that there was little game left for the Indians to hunt.

Some of the tribe urged their chief to destroy the town and drive the intruders off the land which was rightfully theirs. They became aroused to fury when they saw some of the settlers lurking on their land, as if conspiring to grab some more of it. Beating their drums and stamping their feet in a war dance, they were ready to rush against their supposed enemies at the first sign from their chief.

But Han Yerry, sitting at the bonfire with his arms folded, remained silent. At last he stood up and raised his hand.

"I go to Judge White. I will speak with him," he announced.

Judge White lived in a small cabin with his married daughter and a three-year-old grandchild. He met chief Han Yerry with a friendly smile and invited him into the house. After they ate the good food his daughter served, Judge White said, "You came to speak to me, my friend."

The Indian chief nodded his head. "My people are worried that your people want to take more of their land."

"My people want to be friendly with your people. They don't want your land," Judge White said.

"How can we trust them?"

"You have my word," the judge said, extending his hand.

A smile spread over Chief Han Yerry's face. "You are a good man. I trust you," he said, shaking his hand vigorously.

"Come to see me often. And remember we are your friends," Judge White told him as they parted.

Thus reassured, the Indians decided to forget their grudges and live in peace with their pale-faced neighbors. They even learned to like them.

But then came a time when the white settlers in turn became aroused against the Indians. Their horses, one after another, were mysteriously disappearing from their sheds. Who else could have stolen them but the Indians? When a party of settlers came upon two Indians crawling through the tall grass near town, they caught them and locked them up in jail.

Hearing this, Judge White shook his head in disapproval. Once or twice he had seen tough-looking strangers in the town. He intended to find out more about them. Meanwhile, he decided to go to see the two Indians in jail.

"Do you know why you are here?" he asked them. When the two Indians muttered, "no," he continued, "What were you doing in the tall grass near town?"

With difficulty they managed to explain that they were chasing a strayed deer.

"I understand," the judge said, and ordered that they be set free. He took them to his house and, after giving them a good hearty meal, drove them back to their village in his horse and buggy.

The sight of their two braves returning in a horse and buggy aroused much merriment among the squaws and papooses. Shouting and laughing, they rushed toward the buggy. But, seeing that Han Yerry and their braves remained standing aloof, they abruptly drew back.

Puzzled by their gloomy faces, the judge went over to the chief. "I am sorry for what happened. If there is anything else I can do, please tell me."

"My people are angry," the chief replied.

"They say white men cannot be trusted. Their deeds do not speak what their tongues speak. You put our braves in jail and then bring them back in a buggy as though they were women."

Taken aback, for a moment the judge did not know what to say. "I did it out of good will for your people," he tried to assure him.

"I believe you. But my people want better proof of your good will," the chief said, and turned away.

As Judge White drove home he was not happy, but he hoped that the Indians would understand his good intentions and show confidence in him.

The judge did not hear from Han Yerry for some time. Then one day the chief, followed by his squaw, came to visit him. Although it was unusual for the chief to come with his squaw, the judge betrayed no surprise and warmly welcomed them. As they smoked their pipes, he listened to tales of the chief's brave deeds and the many trophies he had collected. The chief promised to show them to him the next time he visited their village. After a while the chief got up to leave.

"I like you and trust you," he said unexpectedly. "Do you trust me?"

"Of course," the judge hastened to reply. "I, too, like you and trust you."

"Then prove it to me with a deed of friendship," the chief said.

"What do you want me to do?" the judge asked.

Pointing at the judge's grandchild, the chief said, "My squaw loves your papoose. She wants to take her to our wigwam and keep her this night. We will bring her back in the morning."

Although shocked by the chief's demand, the judge remained outwardly calm. He knew that to refuse would mean he mistrusted the Indian chief. One never knew what that might lead to. He turned to his daughter expectantly.

Clutching her child close to her, his daughter sat terrified. To trust her little girl to those savages — that was unthinkable! Desperately she pleaded with her eyes not to let the chief take the child away from her. Then, seeing that her father was inclined to yield to the chief's demand, she threw herself at his feet.

"You have nothing to fear from our friends," Judge White tried to reassure his daughter, patting her on the head. Gently taking the

child from her, he handed the little girl to the squaw. "I trust to my friends all that is dearest to me," he said.

The judge and his daughter stayed up all night hoping and praying that nothing dreadful would happen to the child. Time dragged on, and it seemed the night would never end. With the first rays of dawn their anxiety grew more acute. But though they strained their eyes, they saw no one coming down the road. Morning, then afternoon, came and went, and still they waited. In desperation the mother tried to run up the road hoping to detect some sign of her daughter, but the judge held her back. He feared that breaking the trust might cause the death of the child and even the whole town. On the other hand, showing trust in the Indians was the only way to win their friendship.

There was nothing they could do but keep on waiting.

"They are coming!" the child's mother suddenly exclaimed.

Indeed, through the twilight they could see some figures emerging in the far distance and moving toward them. One of them seemed unusually tall, as if wearing a fantastic mask for a special festival.

"I wonder what all this is about," the judge said.

Their eyes were riveted on the procession as it drew nearer.

"There is my child!" the mother cried out, beaming with happiness.

She was not mistaken. Perched on the shoulders of Chief Han Yerry sat her daughter, dressed up in doeskin and bedecked with flowing turkey feathers. She looked like a little Indian princess. Laughing and happy, she was having a grand time.

The Indian chief approached them and, taking the child tenderly off his shoulders, handed her over to her mother. He shook the judge's hand; then, without a word, he and his companions departed.

"You were wise to show trust in the Indians," the judge's daughter later conceded.

As for the Oneida tribe, they always remembered it. From that time on, they did everything they could to help the settlers of Whitesborough and never failed to show their respect for them.

The Oak That Helped Outwit a King

In colonial America, life was rugged and the people were hardy. The land young Samuel Wyllys came to settle on in the colony of Connecticut was a wilderness of trees and brush. It was backbreaking work to clear it. Then there was the job of cutting down trees to build a house. Samuel marveled as he gazed at the trees that surrounded the clearing. He had never seen trees so fine and tall — they seemed to reach the sky.

But of all the trees, the most impressive was the stately oak that stood apart from the others. It was a magnificent tree. Its trunk was stout and its branches spread far in every direction. Its cover of leaves was like a huge umbrella shading the land from the beating sun.

"Out of the wood of this oak I shall be able to make all the things I need to furnish my house," Samuel resolved.

The branches of the forest swayed unconcernedly, caressed by the gentle wind, as Samuel moved among the trees, marking those he intended to cut down. Coming to the oak, he thought he heard a rustle in the bushes, and stopped to listen.

"Must be a deer, or a family of rabbits I frightened," he finally decided, and proceeded to mark the oak.

Day after day Samuel Wyllys kept on chopping down trees, and the sound of his ax rang out over the land. Occasionally a rustling in the bushes would reach his ears, but he no longer paid attention to it.

One morning, armed with his ax, he stopped at the giant oak. He had left it for last, knowing that to chop it down would require a great deal of effort, much more than he had used on the other trees. As he stood considering where to place the first blow of his ax, he again heard a rustle. Turning around, he saw the bushes parting, and some Indians appeared.

Their chief approached him and said, "We have been watching you cut down the trees."

"It's hard work," Samuel said agreeably. Then in a friendly way he asked, "Where do you come from?"

Ignoring his question, the chief pointed at the oak and said, "Do not destroy this tree."

Puzzled, Samuel regarded him. "Why not? It's on my land, isn't it?"

"The land is yours; this tree is ours," the chief replied emphatically. He then told him that the oak was very important to the Indians. As long as they could remember, they had watched for the appearance of its young leaves in the spring, for this was their sign to start planting their corn.

"I understand," Samuel said. "This oak will not be destroyed. I promise you."

The chief's face brightened. "Good," he said, extending his hand. "And promise you will never let your white brothers harm it."

Samuel shook the chief's hand and promised.

Samuel Wyllys seldom saw those Indians again. Soon more colonists came and settled nearby. Before long a new settlement sprang up. Trees were chopped down and land was cleared to make room for more homes.

Only the mighty oak remained standing, spared from the ax. Over the years it had lost its upper branches in winter gales, and lightning had scarred it, leaving a hollow in its trunk. But despite the big cavity, the main trunk went on growing to enormous thickness. In its hollow children played hide-and-seek in the summer and homeless animals found shelter in the winter.

All the time the oak was growing older, the settlement was expanding until it became the city of Hartford. Eventually Hartford became the most important city in Connecticut.

The colony of Connecticut had a charter granted to it in 1662 by King Charles II of England. The people of the colony were happy with the rights and privileges this charter gave them. Then, after Connecticut had been a colony with these charter rights for more than twenty years, the next King of England, James II, suddenly decided to appoint a new governor with absolute power over all of New England.

Wasting no time, the new governor, Sir Edmund Andros, sent a messenger to the New England colonies with an order to surrender their charters. But the people of Connecticut did not want to give up their charter, as they considered the rights it provided to them more precious than gold. Moreover, they thought the charter, being a royal grant, should be respected by the present king.

The people of Hartford were angered. They gathered in groups wondering what to do, and when a messenger came for the charter, they would not give it up. The messenger was forced to return empty-handed. Furious, the governor decided to go to Hartford himself. Arriving there, he went at once to the House of Representatives where the Colonial Assembly was sitting.

One of the men in the Assembly was Captain

Jeremiah Wadsworth. He had a plan for saving the charter, but he needed the cooperation of his fellow representatives. Although no one believed it would work, they nevertheless agreed to help him.

There was dead silence when the governor entered the room and faced the members of the Assembly.

"In the name of our king, I demand that you deliver the charter to me without delay," he ordered.

The governor waited, but the only reply was complete silence. "Bring in the charter!" he thundered.

To the governor's surprise, everybody began talking at once. Some debated the governor's demand, others just talked about anything that entered their minds. Since his voice could not be heard above the din, all the governor could do was wait for them to get tired and stop the silly hullabaloo. The debate grew more heated and the voices rose louder as the day waned. Darkness was creeping into the room and candles had to be lighted.

The charter was finally brought in and placed on the table in full view of everyone present. The voices were stilled, and there was a hush in the room. All eyes were fixed on the governor. Would he simply pick up the charter and walk away with it, leaving them looking foolish? All at once the candles blew out and the darkened room became full of confusion. When the candles were relighted, the charter was gone. There was puzzlement on every face, as everyone pretended not to know who had snatched the charter away.

The crowd that had gathered outside the House rejoiced when they heard that the governor did not get the charter after all.

However, their joy did not last long. For the governor, ignoring the wishes of the people, proceeded to rule much according to his own whims. Still, they were better off than the people of their neighboring colony of Massachusetts. There the governor had taken away the charter and was completely free to rule as he pleased.

Where the charter was hidden remained a mystery for a long time. Although all the Assemblymen were aware that it was Captain Wadsworth who had snatched the charter when the candles were blown out, only a few knew what had actually happened to it. It was Captain Wadsworth's son, waiting outside an open window, who was handed the rescued charter by his father. And it was the son who ran off to hide the precious document in the hollow of the oak tree.

Eventually a squirrel built a nest over the hidden charter and so helped to hide it more securely. There it remained until the American Revolution won independence for the colonies and freed them forever from the rule of kings.

The Charter Oak, which took six people holding hands to encircle it and which was believed to be one thousand years old, is no more. Rain and winds kept crumbling its enormous bulk until a severe storm finally tumbled it. But it is always remembered with pride and affection.

Some of its wood now frames the charter, which is hanging in the state capitol of Connecticut.

As to Samuel Wyllys, he is not forgotten. The hill on which the majestic oak stood is still called Wyllys Hill.

Jonathan Moulton and the Devil

No one in the town of Hampton, in colonial New Hampshire, was as rich as Jonathan Moulton. And no one ever had so great a passion for money. He spent the evenings sitting at his fireplace gloating over his wealth and devising schemes of how to become still richer.

"I would sell my soul to be the wealthiest man in the province," he muttered one evening. The fire was dying down in the fireplace, but Moulton didn't notice it. "Yes, I would sell my soul for it," he repeated dreamily.

A sudden explosion made Moulton sit up with a start. With astonishment he saw a shower of sparks come down the chimney, and from its midst a man elegantly dressed in black velvet stepped out. Even more astonishing was the condition of his clothes. Although the chimney was narrow, they were not in the least disheveled or smudged.

"I am at your service, Moulton," the man said with a low bow. As Moulton just stared at him, he went on, "Let us get on with our business. I am expected at the governor's in ten minutes." To show that he meant what he said, he picked up a red-hot coal and used it as a light to look at his watch.

This was the strangest thing Moulton had ever heard. Portsmouth, where the governor lived, was a long distance away from Hampton. No human being, not even the fastest bird, could possibly cover that distance in such a short time. Gradually the truth began to dawn upon Moulton.

"You are the Devil, aren't you?" he stammered.

"What's in a name?" The man in black laughed. "I heard your offer. Now, is it to be a bargain or not?"

Moulton pricked up his ears. He had always claimed that neither man nor the Devil himself could get the better of him in a trade.

"How can I be sure that you will keep your part of the bargain?" he asked suspiciously.

Giving him a scornful glance, the Devil touched his wig. At once a shower of gold guineas fell to the floor and rolled all over the room.

Greedily Moulton got on his hands and knees to pick them up. But no sooner did he touch them then he had to drop them. The coins were red hot.

Seeing Moulton peevishly getting back to his feet, the Devil chuckled. "Try again," he said. As Moulton shook his head, the Devil urged him on. "Don't be afraid."

Moulton hesitated, but the glitter of the coins made him overcome his caution, and he touched one. To his surprise, the coin was now cool. He weighed it in his hand, then tossed it on the table to hear its ring. There was no doubt — it was a real gold coin.

With a satanic smile, the Devil waited as Moulton crawled over the floor feverishly gathering the coins.

"Are you satisfied?" he demanded when Moulton had finished.

"Yes, indeed," Moulton gasped, still panting from his exertion.

"Now that you are convinced that I can make you the richest man in the province, let us conclude our agreement," the Devil prompted, extracting a paper from his breast pocket. "Now listen: 'I, the Devil, on the first day of every month shall fill your boots in payment for your soul. It shall become the Devil's property forthwith upon the signing of this paper.' Agreed?" Shaking his finger, which glittered with diamonds, he added, "Don't try to play tricks on me. I know you, Moulton, and I shall keep an eye on you."

Still dazed by what was happening, Moulton did not reply.

Not in the least perturbed, the Devil dipped a pen in the inkhorn at his belt and offered it to Moulton.

"'Sign," he demanded, pointing to a blank space on the page already crowded with a variety of flourishing signatures.

Moulton stepped back, wavering.

"If you are afraid, return the money you have pocketed and we will call off the deal."

A hopeful thought that somehow he would manage to get the better of the deal occurred to Moulton. He seized the pen, but before signing stole a glance at the long list of names on the paper. He was amazed to notice how many of the names he knew. "I shall at least be in good company," he mused. Thus encouraged, he finally signed his name.

"Excellent," the Devil said. Taking the paper out of Moulton's hands, he folded it and put it back in his breast pocket. "Now, my friend, be sure you keep faith with me." Then, bowing grandly and flinging his cape about him, he vanished up the chimney.

That night Moulton stayed awake thinking of all kinds of schemes. However, hard as he racked his brain, he could think of no trick clever enough to outwit the Devil. Then he remembered the boots. He examined his own boots and tossed them aside. Even filled to the brim they would not hold enough coins to satisfy him.

The sun hardly began to send out rays to announce its rising when Moulton knocked at the shoemaker's door.

"What can I do for you?" the shoemaker asked, pleased to have such a prominent visitor.

"I need a pair of boots, much larger than the ones I have on, such that would reach up to my thighs," Moulton said.

The shoemaker raised his brows. "Sorry, I don't have such boots," he said. "But maybe I could make you a pair."

Moulton thought it over. He could have boots made that would hold many more coins than his. But then, the Devil might notice that the boots were new and suspect his scheme.

"No, thanks," he said and, cutting the visit short, headed for the blacksmith's shop.

The blacksmith was an enormous fellow. Moulton had seen him at the town fairs towering over the heads of others. Surely his boots would be enormous. The door of the blacksmith shop was open, but he did not enter. He did not have to. From where he stood he could see the boots of the blacksmith, who was busy working at his anvil. They were disappointingly short, hardly reaching halfway to his knees.

Moulton walked off wondering who in town could possibly have the size of boots he wanted. He could think of no one worth the trouble of approaching. Suddenly, seeing a soldier a distance away, he quickened his pace. At closer range the soldier appeared at least as tall as the blacksmith. His boots were long, reaching almost to his thighs.

"Are you a stranger here?" Moulton asked, catching up with him.

"So I am," the soldier replied.

"Could you do me a favor and sell me your boots? I'll pay handsomely for them." Moulton dangled a pouchful of coins before him.

"Now, now," the soldier chided, taken aback. Then, reconsidering, he said, "For so much money I don't mind if I do go barefoot for a while." He took off his boots and handed them over to Moulton in exchange for the pouch of money.

Although the boots were heavy and clumsy, Moulton carried them away with the speed of a young mare. "Ho, there! These are only copper coins you gave me!" he heard the soldier shouting after him. But before the soldier could collect his wits, Moulton had disappeared into his house, secure behind the locked doors.

The Devil kept his promise. On the first day of every month Moulton hung the boots on the crane in the fireplace, and the Devil stuffed them full of guineas.

Moulton became the most prosperous man in the province. Some people envied him, but most of them feared him. "That man would outwit the Devil himself," they grumbled. Hearing it, Moulton smiled to himself — that was precisely what he was planning to do.

One morning the Devil came as usual to fill the boots. But no matter how many coins he poured into them, they remained empty. It was like pouring the money into a bottomless pit.

Puzzled, the Devil decided to come down the chimney to see what was wrong. The chimney was choked up with coins. Enraged, he tore the boots from the crane and examined them. What he saw made him grind his teeth. That conniving Moulton had cut off the soles! And the coins that he had poured into the bottomless boots covered the entire room knee deep!

The Devil uttered a horrible curse and disappeared. That night Moulton's house was burned to the ground. All the precious money Moulton had hidden in the wooden panels of the walls and ceiling disappeared in the fire. Moulton himself escaped with nothing but his nightshirt on.

Watching his house turning into ashes, Moulton wept and tore his hair. Vanishing before his eyes was not only all the gold the Devil had given him, but his own money that he had hoarded for so many years. What would his life be without his wealth? Suddenly it dawned upon him that not all was really lost. His gold coins might have melted, but they could not possibly have turned into ashes. Spurred by his overwhelming desire to rescue his gold, he dashed madly into the burning debris.

Afterward, there was a rumor that someone had seen Moulton coming out of the burning ruins in the company of a man in black, then both disappearing into thin air. One thing was certain — Jonathan Moulton was never seen again.

The Great Scare

Although Windham was a peaceful little town, its people lived in constant fear that something dreadful might happen to them. They never knew what new restrictions the governor of the New England colonies would clamp on them. Nor were they ever safe from attacks by an army of French and Indians. They were well aware that the French had built a chain of forts all the way from New Orleans to Montreal. Obviously the French intended, with the aid of the Indians, to take away land from the English colonies and establish their own rule.

One night in June 1754 the people of that Connecticut town went to bed earlier than usual. Although there had been no rain for many weeks, heavy clouds hung over the town. It was miserably chilly. All the good folk could do was to get under warm quilts to sleep the night away.

A peaceful quiet settled over the little town. Even the miser, who usually stayed up late counting his hoarded money, could not stand the chill. Grudgingly he, too, put on his night-cap and got into bed. Only the smoke from the baker's chimney kept rising into the night. The baker was at his work, for the loaves of bread, the pies and cakes had to be ready by morning. He was a good baker and clever. No one suspected that he gave short weight for their money. At last, his baking done, he also went to bed.

All the people of the town were enjoying their restful sleep when a horrible uproar awakened them and brought them jumping out of their beds. Terrified as the uproar continued, they tried to make out what the noise could be. Not knowing the source of the ghastly sounds made them all the more alarming, and the people were beside themselves with unreasoning fear.

Some thought they could distinctly hear angry war cries and screeches.

"The French and Indians are coming to kill us!" they said.

Others were certain that the Day of Judgment had come. They suddenly remembered all the wrongs they had committed in their lives.

"We deserve the punishment awaiting us," they lamented.

The miser had completely lost his wits. Kneeling at his bed, hands clasped, he prayed, "Oh, Lord, please spare my life. I promise never to be greedy in the future. I will even give some of my hard-earned money to the poor!"

The baker, whose conscience had never troubled him, was also shaking with fear. "I will be honest from now on!" he vowed.

Meanwhile the noise was growing louder and louder. Afraid that the roofs would tumble down on their heads, young and old, barefoot and clad only in their nightshirts, rushed out into the road. Huddling together, they waited and hoped for the terrible noise to stop. From time to time some of them thought they could hear two distinct sounds.

"I hear Colonel Dyer's name!" someone exclaimed.

"Now it's Elderkin!" someone else cried.

Dumbfounded, the people stared in all directions. Dyer and Elderkin were two young lawyers running for town office, and the town was divided, some favoring Dyer, others Elderkin. Surely the Devil must be playing tricks on them for that!

However, there were a few among them who were more level-headed. They asserted that the agitated people were only imagining the calls Dyer and Elderkin. Had the people of Windham forgotten what Indian war cries sounded like? "Let's not deceive ourselves," they warned. "This noise is definitely Indian war cries. We must arm ourselves and go to meet them!"

They scuttled in different directions and soon returned carrying their guns.

"Go back to your homes. We'll call you if we need help," the leader of the volunteers advised the people.

Crawling on their hands and knees and taking cover behind trees and bushes, the volunteers advanced steadily to the hill outside the town where they believed the noise was coming from. There they lay in wait, their eyes straining to detect the enemy.

"The noise is really coming from another direction," their leader finally decided.

They moved to another hill and again lay flat on the ground. But ready as they were to deal with the enemy, they still could find no trace of him. They kept moving to other positions, but without any result. At last, tired and discouraged, they gave up their scouting and returned home.

Meanwhile the townsfolk were standing at their windows anxiously waiting for the brave volunteers to bring them good news. Seeing them lumbering home and looking not at all like conquerers, the good folk became completely discouraged. It was only toward dawn, when the baffling noise had subsided, that the people of Windham allowed themselves a little sleep.

Later in the morning they again poured out into the road. Still mystified by what had happened the night before, they gathered in groups to discuss it. If the noise had really been Indian war cries, what had made the Indians change their minds and leave? On one point they all agreed: they would give a great deal never to have to go through such a horrible experience again.

Just then a man came over the hill, running as fast as his legs would carry him toward the town. All the heads turned in his direction.

"I just saw them! At the pond!" he shouted, wildly waving with his hands, while he was trying to catch his breath.

The people crowded around him, showering him with questions.

"Who? Who? What did you see at the pond?"

"Thousands of them! I — I could hardly believe my eyes!" the man gasped.

They tried to get more sense out of the man, but he kept on repeating, as though in a trance, "I saw them — I swear! Go and see for yourself!"

The people regarded one another uncertainly. No one seemed at all inclined to risk going to the pond. At last a group of men stepped forward and declared that they would brave it.

The millpond was only three quarters of a mile away from town. But because the men thought it wise to be cautious, taking cover and advancing with great stealth, it took them several hours to get there. What they saw explained the mystery of the weird noises.

On both sides of the ditch that ran from the pond, thousands of frogs were lying dead or exhausted. The drought that had stayed on for many weeks had completely dried out the millpond. Only the ditch still retained some moisture. The frogs that thickly populated the pond evidently had wanted to get into the moist ditch. But as there was no room for all, a fierce battle must have occurred as they jostled for a place in the narrow ditch. Due to some strange air condition that night, the piping cries raised by the smaller frogs on one side of the ditch sounded like, "Colonel Dyer!" and the loud rumbling of the bullfrogs from the other side, "Elderkin too!"

Sheepish as the brave men felt, they could

do nothing but go back and tell the people what they had found.

The scare in the town subsided, but it was never forgotten. A poem that was written after that eventful night tells how the people of Windham felt.

Some were well pleased, and some were
mad,
Some turned it off with laughter
And some would never hear a word
About the thing hereafter.
Some vowed that if the De'il himself
Should come, they would not flee him,
And if a frog they ever met,
Pretended not to see him.

As for the miser, although he was tempted to forget his promise, he did give a few coins to the poor.

The baker was more honorable. He fixed his scales properly and never sold his baked goods short weight any more.

Old Meg, the Witch

The people in Gloucester, Massachusetts, suspected that Marget Wesson was a witch. She lived alone in an old house on Back Street, always busy doing something, but no one ever knew what. "Old Meg must be up to some mischief," they would whisper, and shunned her whenever she happened to be walking on the street. Surely many of their misfortunes could be traced directly to Old Meg's doorstep. Hadn't her cat jumped on her neighbor's windowsill miaowing in a weird sort of a way? And hadn't the old man died a couple of days later?

The children were cautioned to keep away from Old Meg for fear that she might cast a spell on them. They usually did. However, sometimes their curiosity got the better of them and they would try to steal a glance at what was going on in the old woman's house.

One morning, when Old Meg was stirring a boiling pot that hung on the crane in the fireplace, she heard a scratching on the window. Wondering what it could be, she went to look. Seeing no one, she returned to her chores. A while later, hearing the noise again, she quickly turned her head to the window. There, plastered against the windowpanes, were the faces of children staring at her with big eyes, as though afraid she was preparing some kind of a devilish brew.

Rushing to the door, she flung it open. "Spying on me, you rascals!" she screamed. The children ran away, mischievously chanting, "Old Meg is a witch!" Angrily she shook her finger at them. "I'll get you, you little devils!" she threatened.

That evening a terrible storm broke out. The sea heaved and the waves mounted, as if the devil himself were lifting them and then tossing them down again. It was difficult for the fishermen in their boats to reach the shore in safety. All were successful except one boy in a small boat, who was lost at sea.

"It was Old Meg!" the children told their elders. "Only this morning she threatened to get even with us!"

Surely the townspeople had other things besides Old Meg to worry about. Gloucester, named after the town in England that had been their home, was a fishing town, and the people lived mostly on what the sea provided. The life of the fisherfolk was hard, and the sea was not always kind to them. Just the same, they loved the sea and accepted what it offered them without complaint.

Their main trouble began when the French took over Louisbourg on Cape Breton Island and fortified it. This in itself wouldn't have mattered much to them; Louisbourg was five hundred miles away from their town. But the French didn't stop at that. They got together a fleet of more than six hundred fishing boats and proceeded to fish and sell their catch along most of the New England coast.

Unable to compete with the French, the Gloucester fishermen found their chances of making a living dwindling. They finally appealed to the governor in Boston to do something about their plight. Full of sympathy for them, the governor at once went into action and mobilized an army of four thousand men to drive the French out of Louisbourg. When he asked the people of Gloucester to contribute some soldiers, they gladly agreed and formed a regiment.

Of course the regiment would not think of beginning its journey on a Friday, for that would be unlucky. Instead they waited till the following Monday. On the eve of their departure the townspeople feasted the soldiers and treated them like heroes. Charms were hung on their necks by mothers and sweethearts in hopes that these would protect them from harm. They were cautioned not to go near haunted houses, while at the same time many a trusting glance was cast at the rusty horseshoes hanging on their houses for luck.

After the banquet the soldiers paraded the streets, saying good-bye to their town. The food and drinks they had consumed put them in a boisterous mood. Their laughter and carrying-on was heard on all the streets — except Back Street, where Old Meg lived. That street was carefully avoided.

But there were two among the soldiers who, in their high spirits, defied all caution and violently knocked on Old Meg's door.

"No need to knock so hard — I'm not deaf," Old Meg grumbled, unlocking the door.

"Wish us good luck," the two soldiers demanded.

Old Meg regarded them suspiciously. "Is that all you want?"

"One more thing. We want you to cast a spell on our enemy," one of the soldiers declared, winking at his companion.

But if their intention was to provoke Old Meg, they failed. "What makes you think I can cast a spell?" she asked.

Their response was a burst of unrestrained laughter. "Everyone in town knows that!"

"They are lying," Old Meg said, still trying to stay calm.

The soldiers shook their heads scornfully. "It is not right for you to be so disrespectful of your townspeople. You are a witch — you cannot deny that."

This was more than Old Meg could bear. "Is that what you came to tell me? Be off and don't ever let me see your dirty mugs again!" she shouted, and shut the door with a bang.

When the regiment finally left, their journey was long and trying. It took them more than a month to reach the colonial army they were to join. Battles with the French followed one after another. The enemy offered stubborn resistance, but the colonial army confidently fought on.

One day the two soldiers who had visited Old Meg back home noticed a crow hovering over their heads. They threw stones at it to drive it away, but the crow kept circling over them persistently and cawing horribly as if threatening them.

"Strange," one of the soldiers said. "I wonder what this means?"

"It means a crow is flying over our heads, you fool," the other soldier replied, trying to make light of it.

They aimed their muskets at the crow and fired, but none of their shots seemed to harm

it. Dropping their muskets, they stood watching the crow hovering over them, not knowing what to do. They were more frightened now than when they faced the French in battle.

"That is not a crow," one of the soldiers muttered.

"Must be an evil spirit in the shape of a crow," the other soldier agreed. Suddenly it dawned upon him. "That's Old Meg, seeking revenge!"

Shooting the evil creature with ordinary bullets, they knew, would be useless. Only silver bullets would have the magic power to kill it. And they had no silver bullets.

"Maybe the silver buttons on our coat sleeves would do the work," the first soldier offered.

They cut off the silver buttons, inserted them into their muskets, then fired. The first button wounded the leg of the crow; the second went straight to its heart. The crow fell to the ground, seemingly dead. Fearing that the crow might come back to life, the two soldiers hurried away from the scene.

The war with the French lasted three

months. In the end the colonial army was victorious. The French were driven out of Louisbourg, to the joy of the Gloucester fishermen.

The Gloucester regiment returned home full of exciting tales about the campaign. But the most curious tale was the one about the crow shot by the two soldiers with silver buttons.

When one of the townspeople heard the tale he inquired, "Exactly when did that happen?" On being told the time, he said, "Why, at that very moment a silver button was being removed from Old Meg's leg! You know, she fell down the stairs in her house and broke her leg. When that leg was examined the silver button was found lodged right there. Soon after, Old Meg died."

All the townspeople shook their heads in amazement. There was not the slightest doubt in their minds now — Marget Wesson had been a witch.

The Goose From Flatbush

There never lived a pirate more daring than Captain Kidd. He led his crew across all the seas, and no ship worth robbing was allowed to pass unchallenged. But like many a pirate, he came to a sad end. At the turn of the eighteenth century he was finally caught and hanged.

No one really knew what happened to all the

treasure Captain Kidd had stolen from ships. But that did not keep people from guessing. Some believed he had buried it somewhere along the Hudson River; others said he had hidden it on Long Island. They all agreed on one point: he had not buried his gold in Flatbush.

Some years after Captain Kidd was gone, there lived a man by the name of Nicholas Van Wemple. His house was in Flatbush, which is across the river from Manhattan. He was far from being a pirate. He was just a fat, henpecked husband. His wife was the ruler of the house, and it was she who held the purse. She never gave him any money except for groceries.

One day before the New Year holiday she told him to hold out his hand. Carefully counting, she put some money into it.

"Go and buy a goose," she said. As he obediently went off, she shouted after him, "Mind you do not stop at the tavern!"

It was a dreary winter day. The ground was icy and the chill went through to Van Wemple's well-covered bones.

As he trudged along the road a strong wind

snatched off his hat. It rolled and rolled until it landed at the tavern's doorstep. Van Wemple picked up his hat and looked longingly at the door of the tavern. "A drink of schnapps would be just right in this weather," he said to himself. But remembering that the only money he had was for the goose, he hesitated. "I'll go in just to warm myself up a bit," he finally decided.

The tavern was full of people drinking, smoking their pipes, and having a jolly good time.

For a moment Van Wemple stood undecided. "It does not look right not to buy at least one drink," he reproached himself. He ordered a schnapps.

Some friends came in and joined him. "Have one on me," offered one friend after another. Van Wemple drank with each one and in turn offered one on him.

The drinks made him drowsy. He put his head on his hands and, before he knew it, was asleep.

Later on, Van Wemple insisted that he had not fallen asleep. He was merely resting his head on his hands when he heard voices coming from the next room. Raising his head, he saw two sailors with black beards and rings in their ears. He could not make out clearly what they were saying. It was something about Captain Kidd ... the old mill on the marshes...

Suddenly he realized what the two sailors were talking about. He waited until they left, then hurried home. No one saw him going into his shed, not even his wife. He took out a shovel and a lantern and headed for the old mill. By then it was pitch dark. The ground was slippery and in some places there was ice cracking under his feet. But he walked on as fast as his stubby legs permitted him.

At last he reached the mill. He knew what he was going to do. Guided by his lantern, he went down to the cellar and began to dig. He tried digging first in one place, then another. On his third try his shovel struck something, and he began to dig harder. Soon he uncovered the top of a canvas bag — a sailor's bag!

Van Wemple tugged with all his strength to pull it out. As he tried to lift it, the canvas tore, scattering gold coins all over the ground. Busily Van Wemple got to work gathering the

coins and filling his breeches and boots with them.

The sound of heavy boots made him look up. Four men stood at the head of the stairs. Two of them he recognized as the sailors from the tavern.

"Look out, good fat friend, don't stow away too many coins, your breeches will burst!" one of the sailors roared. "Come on up and have a drink with us!"

Loaded with gold so that he could hardly move, and scared, Van Wemple somehow managed to climb the stairs. The sailor who had jested with him handed him a jugful of Hollands. "Drink it up!" he commanded.

The men waited till he emptied the jug to the last drop. Then, turning him upside down, they shook out all the coins from his breeches and boots. Setting him upright, they grabbed him by his breeches and threw him out the window.

For a while Van Wemple lay in mud and icy water unable to move. At last, summoning all his strength, he got himself to his feet and staggered away from the mill.

What happened to him afterward he did not

remember until he was awakened by the screaming voice of his wife. Sitting up, he blinked his eyes and tried to collect his wits. But it took him some time to realize that he was sitting in the snow close to his house, holding on to a plucked goose.

"Now, where did I get this plucked bird?" he asked himself.

Gradually it all came back to him. As the sailors grabbed him to throw him out the window, he had clutched something, trying to save his life. It must have been this plucked goose! The sailors had probably stolen it for their own New Year's feast.

"Here is your goose," Van Wemple said triumphantly, handing it over to his wife.

"You call this skinny thing a goose? And it took you such a long time to bring it?" she grumbled. "Now, don't go on sitting in the snow or you'll catch your death of cold. Get into the house!"

In the house before a warm fire Van Wemple told his wife what happened to him. To that tale she rolled her eyes upward, as if asking the heavens to have mercy on her husband.

"You found gold? Well, where is even one coin to prove it?"

"How did I get the goose then? I had no money," he argued. But his wife had not the patience to listen to him any longer. "You brought it, that's all I care about," she said, and went to attend to her goose.

Some days later, Van Wemple told his tale to his friends at the tavern. They merely laughed at the whole story. "Captain Kidd's treasure buried in Flatbush? Whoever heard of such a thing!"

No one to this day believes that there is or ever was hidden treasure in Flatbush. But some people do point out spots along the Hudson, particularly Cro'Nest at Storm King Mountain, as likely places where one might find the loot Captain Kidd buried long ago.

As to how Nicholas Van Wemple obtained his goose, that riddle was never solved.

A Happening on Christmas Eve

It was a quiet Christmas Eve in Michael Kuch's little house at Valley Forge. The supper finished, old Kuch and his daughter sat at the fireplace cheerlessly watching the burning logs. Outside, the ground around the house was covered with a blanket of untouched snow. But it was different farther away. There the snow was gray and muddied by marching troops.

"Don't worry, Father. By next Christmas the war will be over and Willy will be back home with us," the daughter was saying.

"I wonder," old Kuch muttered.

Seeing gloom on her father's face, the girl tried to comfort him. "You know Willy is under the command of General Washington himself. Surely he'll be safe with him."

Old Kuch didn't reply, and time dragged on until the clock struck twelve.

"We had better offer our prayer for the safety of my son and go to bed," he said at last. He was about to bank the fire in the fireplace when he heard running steps in the crunching snow, then violent knocking on the door. Putting down the poker, he went to unlatch it. It was flung open and their young neighbor rushed into the room all disheveled and panting. He sank into a chair and nervously began to wring his hands.

"What's happened, John?" the girl asked, bending over him. Getting no response and seeing him shaking, she turned to her father, pleading with her eyes for help.

"Now compose yourself, son," old Kuch said gently. "Tell us, what's wrong?"

With great effort, still shaking and frightened, John revealed that he had tried to kill General Washington. The bullet had missed him but struck his attendant, a dragoon. "Please hide me. They are on my track now," he pleaded.

Taken aback, Kuch just regarded his young neighbor for a few moments. "John Blake," he said finally, "although my boy is with the troops, I'm neutral in this war. You know that, don't you?"

"Father — !" the girl urged, touching his arm.

Gently pushing her hand aside, he continued, "It was a cowardly thing you did. You Tories don't fight like men — that's what I have against you. But since my daughter likes you, for her sake I'll do what you ask me. Follow me to the spring house."

Kuch had hardly returned to his waiting daughter when the door was flung open and some soldiers in blue and buff stormed into the room.

"We want the assassin," their spokesman demanded.

Kuch raised his brows. "What leads you to

think there's an assassin in my house?"

"His tracks in the snow. Come on, bring him out."

But Kuch, sinking into his chair, folded his arms and kept silent. The soldiers scrambled about the house looking into every corner, upturning quilts and baskets, and even poking into the oven. Finding nothing, they returned to the main room.

"Now, enough playing the innocent fool. Where is he?" their spokesman barked, grabbing old Kuch by the collar of his coat and forcing him out of his chair. Raising his hand, he was about to strike him when a tall, stately man came through the open door. He was carrying a soldier who seemed to be lifeless. "Leave the man alone," he ordered.

"Yes, General," the soldier replied, and let go of Kuch.

Gently, as though handling a sick child, General Washington put the bleeding body down on the warm floor at the fireplace. "This man is badly wounded." He shook his head. Nevertheless he told the girl to warm up some water.

As the general stepped aside and the fire

from the burning logs lit up the face of the wounded man, Kuch cried out, “My son!” Sobbing, he fell on his knees and embraced him. His sobbing stopped shortly and it seemed as if both father and son were lifeless. Presently he got to his feet and looked about the room wildly. The pistol the assassin had dropped when entering was still lying in the shadow cast by the chair on the floor. Kuch picked it up and, before the soldiers could stop him, sprang to the door and headed for the spring house.

At first he could see nothing in the darkness of the spring house.

“Come out of your hiding place, John Blake! I'll make you pay for the murder of my son if it's the last thing I do!” he raved. Detecting the figure of the fugitive crouching in the shadows in the far corner, he growled and, aiming his pistol, fired. But the bullet landed far from the mark, as the pistol was knocked out of his hand by his daughter, who reached the scene just in time. Enraged, Kuch pulled out his knife. “Come out, you coward!” he shouted.

Out of the darkness John Blake came,

crouching, and dropping on his knees, bared his chest.

"Don't do it, Father! Don't, for my sake!" the girl cried.

If she didn't soften her father's heart, she did succeed in postponing his mad deed long enough for the soldiers to reach the spring house. Seizing the fugitive, they dragged him back to the house and made him confront the general.

"What do your countrymen call you?" Washington asked him.

"John, John Blake," was the meek reply.

Washington regarded him scornfully. "What puzzles me is, what harm have your countrymen done to you that you should so turn against them?"

Blake hung his head. "I'm willing to die," he muttered.

Washington waved that off with his hand. "We could use spirited young men like you. He is your neighbor, isn't he?" He pointed at the lying man.

As Blake turned toward the man he shot, his face brightened. "He is alive!" he exclaimed, trembling with excitement.

"You are a poor shot; that was lucky for you," Washington said. Indeed, there was no doubt that the wounded man was alive. For he opened his eyes and tried to lift himself. "Father," he called.

At that moment old Kuch trudged in with his daughter and stopped at the door, perturbed by the cheerful faces in the room. "Willy is calling you, Father. He will live!" the girl cried out. Father and daughter rushed to their loved one, each taking turns embracing him.

Washington waited till they had a chance to let their feelings flow. Turning to the prisoner, he said, "You, too, are not ready to die. But you will be watched." Then, addressing the girl, he said, "I will leave him in your custody. Try to make an American of him."

The evening that had started so cheerlessly was now full of joyous promise. Old Kuch could not find words adequate enough to thank the general for saving his son's life.

"I did for your son no more than he would do for me," he said. The clock striking one brought mock alarm to his face. "It is getting late, in fact it is now Christmas morning, my good man. May I wish you all good health and happiness."

Standing at the door, old Kuch and Blake watched the general ride away with his soldiers until they disappeared in the early morning mist.

"There's a leader worth following," old Kuch said.

"Maybe you're right," Blake replied thoughtfully.

A great change took place in John Blake. When young Kuch recovered, Blake eagerly joined him in the same regiment, and no soldier served Washington more bravely than he did. And when the war was over and Blake married the girl and they had children, there was no family happier than the one around old Kuch.

The Part-time Prisoner

When the Indians first met the early settlers of the New England colonies they were surprised at how loud and talkative they were. *Yanokies* — the quiet ones — they named them jokingly. And Yankees they were called from then on.

Nathan Jackson was a typical Yankee. Although his face was weather-beaten and etched with deep lines, there was always a twinkle in his eyes, and he enjoyed a good hearty laugh. Tall and lanky with broad shoulders, he was used to hard work. His neighbors respected him for his honesty.

However, there was one thing about him his neighbors could not accept — he was a Tory. He didn't try to hide this fact. On the contrary, he openly declared it, firmly believing that in the long run the King of England's rule would be best for the colonies. But, while regretting the stand he took, they didn't resent him. "Let him think what he wishes as long as he doesn't cause us any trouble," they said.

But there came a time when their village was threatened by the English redcoats. The villagers put up stout resistance — except for Nathan Jackson. Convinced that his countrymen were wrong in being disloyal to the king, and following his own conscience, he joined the redcoats.

Greatly outnumbered, the villagers would have been destroyed if it had not been for the colonial troops that came to their help. In the end the English were driven away and Nathan Jackson was captured. Charged with treason, he was put in jail in Great Barrington, Massachusetts, to be eventually brought to trial.

The people of Great Barrington were for the most part honest and neighborly, and crime among them was practically unknown. Their jail was so little used that in time it became a mere shed hardly fit for keeping anyone locked up.

"You call this chicken coop a jail?" Nathan Jackson's laughter pealed out, as the sheriff was locking him up. "Why, I can just walk out of here whenever I please!"

The sheriff looked frightened. "You wouldn't do that to me, would you, Jackson?"

"Now don't worry, my friend," Jackson assured him. "And don't lose any sleep on my account. I'm staying right here. You have my word for it."

Jackson kept his word and made no attempt to escape. But as time went on he found life in the shed too monotonous.

"Couldn't you find something for me to do?" he pleaded with the sheriff one day. As the sheriff stared at him blankly he said with a twinkle, "Put some chickens or maybe a cow in this shed for me to take care of. That'll give me something to do."

"There's no room for them," the sheriff objected.

"Then let me go out and do an honest day's work and I'll come back to sleep in jail. I promise I will."

The sheriff scratched his head as he thought it over. He was aware Jackson was not bluffing, as he knew his reputation for honesty. "This has never been done, you know," he said at last. "But I think it's all right."

This arrangement proved agreeable to both the sheriff and the prisoner. At sunrise the sheriff showed up to unlock the shed and was free of his duty of attending to the prisoner for the rest of the day, and Jackson went back to take care of his small farm. At sunset Jackson returned, and all the sheriff had to do was to lock him up and go home.

One day Jackson, returning to prison for the night, found it locked and the sheriff nowhere around. Having nothing better to do, he decided to take a walk along the road. He finally saw the sheriff lumbering toward him.

"Sorry," the sheriff said. "You know it's harvest time. I hope I didn't inconvenience you."

"That's all right," Jackson replied cordially.

But the following day the sheriff arrived at the shed earlier than usual. He looked worried. "I've just received word to take you to Springfield to stand trial for treason," he grumbled.

"When do we start?" Jackson asked.

The sheriff threw up his hands. "How can I go? Don't they know this is harvest time?"

Smiling, Jackson put a hand on the sheriff's shoulder to comfort him. "You don't need to bother taking me all the way to Springfield. I'll walk there by myself. I don't mind."

The sheriff's face melted into a broad smile. "You'd be doing me a great favor," he said.

Springfield, where the big prison was, was fifty miles away from Great Barrington. Jackson walked unhurriedly, stopping now and then to examine the unbroken soil along the road, or to watch a passing flock of birds. "This may be my last walk as a free man; I might as well enjoy it," he thought. He spent the night in the open field marveling at the immense dome with countless twinkling stars over his head. In the morning he resumed his walking. Occasionally he met with travelers on horseback, or a farmer with a wagonful of produce prompting his horse on to some marketplace. A carriage carrying a well-dressed gentleman overtook him, then stopped.

"Would you care to have a lift, stranger?" the gentleman offered.

"Thanks just the same, but I kind of like walking," Jackson said. Then, as his hand rested on the carriage seat and felt its softness, he changed his mind. "Oh, well, I guess I wouldn't mind getting such a lift," he said.

"Where are you bound for?" the gentleman asked when Jackson was seated beside him.

"Springfield, to stand trial," Jackson said.

"Farmland trouble?"

"Not for that kind of trifle. It's for treason."

The gentleman regarded him with astonishment. "Who are you?" Without hesitation Jackson gave his name. "And are you walking to Springfield to give yourself up?"

"Well, I wouldn't put it exactly that way," Jackson said. He told him that actually he had been caught when he tried to help the English, and had been put in prison, or rather a chicken coop. He explained the sensible arrangement he had made with the sheriff. He also told him about the predicament of that poor sheriff when he had thought he would have to neglect his harvest to escort his prisoner to Springfield.

They traveled on in silence, except that the gentleman kept muttering to himself and shaking his head. Reaching the outskirts of Springfield, he drew on the reins. "Here is where you get off," he said.

"How far are you going?" Jackson asked.

"Boston. Good luck to you," the gentleman said, and drove off.

Jackson headed directly for the courthouse and gave himself up. A few weeks later he was tried and sentenced to death.

While he was awaiting execution the Executive Council was meeting in Boston. They were reviewing petitions for clemency for sentenced criminals that they had received from all over the New England colonies.

"Are there any petitions in favor of a man named Nathan Jackson?" Mr. Edwards, one of the councilmen, wanted to know. They went through the pile of petitions. There were none that dealt with Nathan Jackson.

"That condemned man deserves mercy,"

Mr. Edwards declared. He then went on to tell an extraordinary tale about the amazingly honest man to whom he had given a lift.

A murmur of surprise and admiration for the condemned man went around the room. A letter was hurriedly sent to Springfield which arrived just in time to prevent his execution. Instead, the prison door was opened and Nathan Jackson walked out a free man.

Chief of the Night Riders

No one would deny that John Blake had a fine farm, least of all he. He was one of the first men to brave the hardships of settling among the Berkshire Hills in Massachusetts. It was hard work to turn the wilderness into good farming land, but he had patience. He had to admit, however, that if it had not been for the help and good will of his neighbors he wouldn't have succeeded as well as he had. In time, more settlers came and joined him to form a fine and happy community. That is — until old Francis Woolcott came to live with them.

Where the old man had come from no one knew. He was tall and bony. He had horrible protruding teeth, and his mousey eyes were constantly shifting as though they were set on wires. His laugh was harsh enough to give one a chill.

There was talk among the farmers that Francis Woolcott was really the chief of thirteen night riders whose faces no one had ever seen. Some of the farmers even seemed to know that Woolcott was meeting the night riders in the ash grove every night when the moon was high in the sky. They came with bundles of stolen straw which Woolcott changed into black horses. Carrying the night riders with lightning speed, the horses leaped over bushes, fences, and even trees without the slightest effort. Following their chief's command, the night riders galloped about the country doing mischief. Then, at the stroke of midnight, the riders disappeared and the horses changed back to straw as if nothing had happened.

John Blake had a pair of well-fed, strong horses of which he was quite proud. One day he harnessed them up to plow his field.

"Giddap!" he called to them.

It was a joy to see how easily they pulled the plow and a pleasure to smell the freshly turned-up earth. Suddenly the horses stopped.

"Giddap, giddap!" he prompted them. But the horses wouldn't budge. Blake cracked the whip as a warning and, when that didn't help, slashed them with it. Still the horses wouldn't move; they didn't even seem aware of the slashing they were getting. Blake tried to coax them and pull them, but it was of no avail. Exasperated, the farmer stopped to puzzle out what was wrong with his horses. Then he heard a loud, mocking laugh. He turned around, and there was old Woolcott leaning against a tree.

"What are you doing on my land?" the farmer yelled out, his annoyance at his horses now transferred to the intruder.

Still laughing, the old man advanced toward the farmer.

"A fine pair of horses you have," he chuck-

led. Then, wiping his protruding teeth with his sleeve, he added slyly, "Maybe they'll be more willing to work if you give me some cider and a bit of salt pork."

Blake didn't argue. He didn't know whether to believe all the strange things people were saying about the old man. As he saw it, Woolcott was just a scheming old crank. Still, there had to be some reason why the farmers feared him and gave him everything he asked for. Better to be on the safe side, he thought.

"Come to my house," he said.

Later, returning to the field, he was surprised to see his horses turning their heads toward him as though impatient to get going. Sure enough, no sooner did he touch the reins than the pair started off with more energy than ever.

John Blake never told his neighbors or even his wife about the strange behavior of his horses, but he thought about it a great deal. He finally decided that his suspicions were nonsense, and dismissed them from his mind.

He was having supper one evening when farmer Raught's wife came hurrying into the house, looking as though she had lost her mind.

"Are you all right, neighbor?" Blake asked, concerned.

"Nothing wrong with me — it's our pigs!" she moaned.

Blake raised his brows. Pigs were something to worry about. But he didn't think pigs were worth getting so terribly upset about, not even the best of them.

"What's the trouble with your pigs?" he wanted to know.

"I would never have believed it, but my husband saw them with his own eyes. Oh, heavens!" she went on moaning.

"Talk sense," Blake demanded.

It took a good while before the woman could compose herself enough to tell what had happened. Her husband had been working around the shed when he suddenly stopped, dumbfounded. Before him was the queerest sight imaginable. His pigs were walking on their hind legs, bowing and shaking each other's forelegs and behaving just like human beings. They were even trying to talk like human beings. Farmer Raught rubbed his eyes, at first refusing to believe what he saw. But, as sure as he was a sinner, the pigs went on parading on their hind legs, just like real human folks.

"He was so unnerved that he developed a fever and was obliged to get into bed," the woman asserted.

Blake listened with a doubtful twinkle in his eyes. Nevertheless he got up, saying, "I'll go and take a look at your pigs."

When he returned home a while later, his wife met him with a worried face.

"Well, what did you see?" she prompted him.

"Pigs sleeping and wallowing in mud," he said shortly.

His wife gave an exasperated sigh. "That old Woolcott *would* play that kind of nasty trick on innocent folk."

"Now, don't go around saying that unless you have proof," Blake barked back at her.

Blake's wife didn't argue any further. She was sure that sooner or later her husband was bound to learn the truth about old Woolcott.

However, farmer Blake had more pressing

things to think about. His wheat field was ready to be harvested, and he could use some help. With this in mind he went to see farmer Williams.

The dirt road that led to Williams' farm cut through the woods. Although the woods were usually alive with roaming animals, that afternoon they kept a mysterious silence. There was not even the rustle of a rabbit, nor the sound of a bird calling its mate.

"Hup, hup, hup!" suddenly came resounding through the woods. Blake looked around, perturbed. No animal could have made such sounds. But the trees stood still, betraying nothing.

Approaching Williams' farm, Blake again heard "Hup, hup, hup!" coming from a distance. "What on earth could that be?" he wondered. Seeing Williams and his wife at the door of their house, frantically motioning to him, he quickened his steps.

"Anything wrong?" he asked.

Speechless, they pointed into the house.

Blake peeped inside the open door and what he saw sent a chill through him. The five Williams children were skipping from one chair to another as though they were birds. "Hup, hup, hup!" they chanted. But more astonishing still was to see them leap to the molding on the walls, which was hardly an inch wide, and then run around and around the room.

"Stop it!" Blake shouted. But before he could do anything else, farmer Williams and his wife pulled him away from the door.

"The evil spirit of old Woolcott got into them. It will get tired after a while and leave of its own accord," they whispered.

"What makes you think it's old Woolcott's doings?" Blake queried.

"Who else could it be? He's done plenty of mischief, everybody knows that."

Blake shrugged his shoulders and stood by until the children quieted down. As that was no time to ask Williams to give him a hand in harvesting his field, he decided to come another time.

Strange things went on happening among the Berkshire Hills. One farmer found his horses' tails tied, another saw his pigs walking backward. Some of the farmers insisted that their wheat fields were trampled by the night riders. They even observed shadows cast by their leaping horses. And who had not heard old Woolcott's sinister laughter on the mornings after the night riders had done their mischief?

Francis Woolcott was over ninety years old and, the way he was carrying on, it seemed he was going to live forever. However, one day Williams unexpectedly showed up at Blake's farm.

"Looks as if the Devil has at last come to claim old Woolcott," he announced.

"No need to be so hard on him," Blake reprimanded him.

Knowing that the dying old man was alone, he decided to go and stay at his bedside, and persuaded Williams to come along.

They had been at the bedside only a short time when a storm broke out. As the storm rumbled, the old man's face twisted and then became so horrible that the farmers shuddered and moved away to the door. A purplish-blue flame burst at the window followed by a thunderous clap; there was a smell of sulphur, and old Woolcott was dead.

When the two farmers left the cabin, to their surprise the sky was clear and the moon was shining brightly. The ground was dry, and there was not the slightest indication that there had been a storm only a few minutes before.

"I always maintained that Francis Woolcott was an evil spirit that had taken human shape," Williams said.

Blake nodded his head — he finally had to agree with him.

The Mystery of Pelham House

In Pelham, Massachusetts, near the road that led to Pelham Bridge stood a quaint old house. Its doors were bolted, for no living person wanted to stay in it. The townspeople believed that once a young woman, Anne Hutchinson, had lived in a cabin nearby. When Indians killed her and her entire family and burned their cabin, for a time her spirit hovered over the smoldering ashes. Then her spirit, seeking shelter, moved into the bolted house to mourn her lot and to terrify the old women in the neighborhood with all kinds of pranks.

The young man who inherited Pelham House lived most of the time in the big city. Being an adventurous young man and not believing in spirits, he wanted to reopen the house. But hard as he tried, he could not get a caretaker from the neighborhood. Even those he brought from far away would not remain more than a day or two. Frightened by what they saw and heard during their stay, they spread strange tales about the old house.

Equally strange were the tales of the teamsters who happened to pass the house late at night on their way to town. Some saw a light moving from room to room and heard a woman crying as though she were being pursued. Others claimed they saw the house all lit up. Still others saw the house violently shaking, as though invisible hands were trying to pull it off the ground.

It was no wonder that the townspeople were troubled when they heard of the young owner's reckless intention to come and live in the house. They urged him to change his mind — to stay away from it and, if anything, add another lock. To their dismay the young owner merely laughed. "I'll risk it," he said.

It was early in the spring when he offered a farmer and his wife from another province the opportunity to come and take care of the house. The couple had only a vague idea what the house was like, and being badly in need of work they readily accepted the offer. They were pleasantly surprised to find the inside of the house well fitted up with good old Dutch-style furnishings. They were especially pleased with the fireplace, which was decorated with fine old Dutch tiles.

"Quite different from the ramshackle home we had!" the farmer's wife observed with a contented sigh.

Wasting no time, she went ahead cleaning up the house, while the farmer attended to the overgrown garden. There were heavy layers of rotting leaves, which had accumulated over many years, to cart away and dried-up brush to get rid of. The sun had made its full round in the sky when the farmer finally decided he had done enough work for the day.

The couple went to bed early. Although they heard some rumbling in the house, they were too tired to pay any attention to it.

The following morning the farmer went out again to work in the garden. He noticed that the teamsters whipped up their horses when passing the house. That was odd, he thought. Were they trying to let him know that he, being a stranger, was not welcome in the community?

It was noontime when his wife came running out of the house looking alarmed. "The doors of all the rooms keep opening and closing all on their own!" she called to him.

"That doesn't make sense," the farmer grumbled. Nevertheless, he followed her into the house. He went through all the rooms, but found everything quiet. "Must have been a sudden wind that caused it." He shrugged, and went back to work.

During the evening meal no mention was made of her alarm. When darkness set in they went to bed and fell asleep immediately.

In the middle of the night the farmer's wife sat up with a start and shook her husband

awake. "Did you hear that noise?"

"What noise? What did you hear?" he asked.

"Babies crying something awful."

"You must have been dreaming," the farmer complained, and pulled the quilt over his head.

He had hardly fallen asleep when his wife shook him again. "There they go, crying again," she whispered.

The farmer listened, puzzled at the sound. "There must be an owl's nest in one of the trees. I'll find it tomorrow. Now try to sleep."

But the farmer's wife did not close her eyes that night. She was certain it was not owls but babies crying.

The farmer did not bother to look for the owl's nest. A person was bound to hear strange noises in a country he was not familiar with, he reasoned. Just the same, when night came and he was ready to go to bed, he put a lighted lantern at his bedside. He tried to stay awake, but he was tired from the day's work and soon fell asleep.

It was close to midnight when a deafening bang woke him up. He saw his wife sitting up, terrified.

"Don't say I'm dreaming this time," she breathed.

The farmer had to agree that she was not dreaming. Doors kept creaking and banging as they opened and closed. It seemed as if a wild party was going on, and the guests were rushing from room to room having a hilarious time. Topping this noise came a crash as though all the dishes in the house were thrown to the ground.

The farmer remembered that the young owner of the house had stored his dishes in one of the rooms. Bracing himself, he picked up the lantern and went to see what was going on there. He found the room in good order. The dishes that had been piled up on a table were still there and not a single one was broken.

For a while he stood rubbing the back of his neck. "Now, what on earth could have caused that awful crash?" he kept asking himself. "And those doors banging?" He stepped out into the garden, expecting to meet with stormy weather. But the sky was dotted with stars and there was not a breeze. "Well," he tried to reassure himself, "there's really nothing strange about the doors. All they need is fixing so that they close properly."

The farmer spent another full day of work. After supper he sat before the warm fire to think about the house. What did he know about it? Perhaps he should make a thorough search.

While he was thinking this, the wall in front of him slowly opened and a vapory shadow moved into the room. As it moved on, it gradually formed into a human figure. And when it reached the middle of the room he could clearly see all the features of a girl. She was young and graceful, and her long dark hair was streaming down over her shoulders. Her face was beautiful, but full of sorrow. She stood for a moment silently regarding him. Then, gliding across the room, she disappeared through the opposite wall.

Thoroughly shaken up though he was by what he had seen, he decided not to tell his wife about it. That night they were not troubled by any noise. But as soon as the sun rose the farmer woke his wife.

"Pack our things. I have had enough of this house," he said with finality.

That morning they locked up the house and left.

The house was never reopened. No more did the teamsters, speeding past the house, notice any flickering lights coming from it. But some occasionally claimed they had seen a girl leaning on her elbows and mournfully looking out of a window of Pelham House.

The White Deer of Onota

Once a band of Indians crossed the Berkshire Hills of Massachusetts and settled near the shores of Lake Onota. The men hunted in the surrounding forests and the women raised maize, but they did not fare well. The game in the forests was scarce and the maize grew poorly. The winter was especially trying; the snow lay heavily on the ground and food was scarce. Some of the men, disheartened, urged that they abandon their wigwams and move to kinder lands.

One late afternoon an Indian came running to the village shouting, "There is a white deer drinking at the lake!"

The Indians of the village had heard amazing tales about white deer, but they had never seen one. Headed by their wise man, they hurried to the lake. Indeed, on the opposite side of the lake there stood a deer whiter than the whitest snow. Magnificent antlers, glowing like a crown of amber, adorned his head. The deer looked up at the gathered Indians as if greeting them, then went on drinking undisturbed.

"What does this mean?" the Indians asked eagerly, crowding around their wise man.

"This is a good omen," the wise man replied gravely. "So long as the white deer drinks at our lake no famine shall touch us nor sickness visit our wigwams."

The Indians returned to their village much cheered by their wise man's prophecy. And when later they saw the deer with a doe as white as himself coming to the lake to drink, their spirits rose still higher.

That summer the maize grew unusually tall and plentiful. The hunters, too, had much better luck. By the time fall came their wigwams were stacked full with fine furs.

There was much rejoicing in the village. To celebrate their good fortune they arranged feasts such as they never had before. Nor did they neglect to honor the wise man for his wonderful prophecy.

They were not worried about selling their furs. Surely a fur trader would show up before long. And when a fur trader did appear, they treated him as though he were an expected and welcome guest.

"Stay with us awhile and rest before you journey back to your faraway homeland," they urged.

The fur trader readily agreed. For the longer he stayed, the better bargain he hoped to make with these out-of-the-way Indians.

The following morning the fur trader, refreshed by a good night's rest, wanted to see the beautiful Lake Onota he had heard so much about. The wise man, who was also the chief of the village, agreed to lead him to it.

The early mist was lifting above the lake when they reached its shore.

"There is a white deer!" the fur trader exclaimed, pointing to the other side of the lake.

The wise man nodded his head proudly. "He comes here every day to drink."

"What a rare animal!" the fur trader breathed. "I want his hide!"

As the Indian turned his head away and didn't reply he urged, "For that deerskin I'll pay you as much as all your furs are worth."

The chief's eyes flared with anger. "This animal is sacred. It brings us good fortune. It must not be harmed!"

Knowing that it would be unprofitable for him to arouse suspicion in this Indian, the fur trader quickly dropped the matter.

However, back in the village he went on thinking about the amazing white skin of the deer he had seen at the lake. He resolved to get it no matter what it cost him.

He needed someone to help him, but dared not ask anyone in the Indian village. Suddenly a bright thought occurred to him — he would ask Wondo the drunk! That degenerate would

sell his soul for a copper penny.

He found Wondo sitting under a tree, dozing. "Wondo," the fur trader whispered into his ear. As Wondo opened his eyes, he dangled some money before him. "It's all yours and more if you will help me."

"I'll do what you say," Wondo muttered, eagerly reaching for the money.

The fur trader told him what he wanted him to do. Wondo was to get the hide of the white deer and meet him next morning on the trail he was going to take to travel back home.

Wondo did what he was expected to do. He brought the snow-white skin to the arranged place and got an additional sum of money.

"Don't ever go back to the village — they'll kill you," the fur trader cautioned him as they parted.

No longer did the white deer come to the lake to drink. Gloomily the Indians of the village sat in their wigwams wondering what wrong they had committed that had caused the white deer and his doe to leave them. In their grief they were not aware that Wondo had disappeared. But one day one of the Indians came running to the village, angrily waving his spear as though calling for war. He had just come upon the remains of the white deer in the woods.

"The sacred deer has been killed!" he told the gathered Indians. Shocked by the news, they stood silent with their heads bent.

"Wondo is gone," someone spoke up.

It suddenly became clear to everybody that no one but Wondo could have committed that terrible crime.

"The killing of the sacred deer shall be avenged," the wise man declared, raising his hands to the sky.

That fall, heavy threatening clouds constantly hung over the village. The water in the lake overflowed its bounds, for no deer came to drink it. The winter arrived with fury, sending biting frost into the wigwams and heavy snow whirling over the village. The Indians shivered, and no fire was warm enough to drive away the cold. They could do nothing but patiently wait for the winter to wear itself out and leave. Spring came late, but at last they could resume their hunting and plant their maize.

It happened that one day an English hunter

followed by his dog wandered away from his companions and came to the shore of Lake Onota. For a while he stood admiring the lake; he had never seen such a beautiful stretch of water. As he started to retrace his steps to his camp, he saw a white doe moving among the foliage. Much excited over his good fortune in coming upon such an unusual doe, he waited for the right moment to aim at it with his gun. But as he put his finger on the trigger, ready to shoot, his dog suddenly let out a terrific howl. The bullet that went off missed the doe. Angered, the hunter gave the dog a scolding and commanded it to keep still. Again he lifted his gun and aimed at the doe, and again the dog let out a howl as he fired, as though the gun were aimed at him. Meanwhile the doe stood watching them, unharmed and not the least disturbed. Then, with great dignity, she slowly walked away.

Now the hunter was frightened. Was the white doe really an animal? Or was it a spirit that had taken the shape of an animal and bewitched his dog? It must be a good spirit if it took the shape of a beautiful doe, he finally decided. Thus reassured, he started to walk away when his path was blocked by a group of Indians. They had heard his shots and wanted to know what he was doing on their land.

The hunter explained that he had lost his way. He also told them that he had come upon a strange animal, a white doe. Usually he was a good shot, but this time his bullets went wide of the mark. Worse than that, his shots had sent terror into his dog.

Angered by his tale, the Indians seized him and were ready to harm him, but their wise man stopped them.

"Which way was the doe moving when you saw her?" he demanded.

"She seemed to be heading for the lake," the hunter said.

The wise man unexpectedly grabbed his hand and shook it heartily. "You bring us good tidings," he exclaimed. "This white doe is sacred. Our good fortune has returned!"

"I am glad it turned out this way," the hunter replied.

After he had promised never to harm their sacred animal, the Indians escorted him to his camp.

Back in his camp, the hunter told his companions about his encounter with the white doe. They laughed at him, and said they did not believe in dreams.

"Sometimes a beautiful dream can become real," the hunter replied, and glanced wistfully at his dog. If only his dog could talk!

Kayutah, the Drop Star

Their daughter was three years old when the Carters settled near the Genesee River in western New York. They had a hard time at the beginning. The country they came to was a wilderness. They had to cut down trees to build their home. The land had to be cleared of brush and stones to make it fit for planting corn and other vegetables. Then there was the constant fear that the Indians might attack them or set their home on fire.

The first winter was especially difficult. Food was scarce. The ground was buried under deep snow. There were no roads, and the nearest settler was a long distance away.

But then spring came. The trees donned their green buds and flowers blossomed along the riverbank. It was time for planting.

"Our little daughter will be as pretty as a lily when she grows up," Mrs. Carter said as she worked in the field beside her husband. She glanced contentedly in the direction of their house, expecting to see her daughter playing in front of it. But the little girl was not there. "I told her to stay close to the house," the mother grumbled, and went to find her daughter.

The child was not in the house, nor anywhere near it. "Where could she have wandered off to?" her mother thought, worried. Then she remembered the path that led to the riverbank. Following the path, she searched behind every bush until she came to the river. There was her little daughter, leaning far out over the steep bank trying to reach a flower.

"Don't do that!" the mother cried and, rushing over, pulled her away from the dangerous spot. "You could have fallen into the river and there would have been no one around to save you, you silly child!" She made her daughter promise to stay close to the house in the future.

Evidently her little daughter did not keep her promise. For one day when she returned from the field to make lunch for the family, the mother did not find her at the house.

"I suppose she's gone off to pick flowers again!" the mother muttered, and hurried to the riverbank. Her daughter was not there. Panicky, she ran back to the field. "I am afraid our daughter has drowned!" she cried.

"Nonsense," Carter said. "Must have just wandered off. We'll find her."

They searched the riverbank, the woods, then the river, but found no trace of their little daughter that day, nor the next. For weeks and months they searched before the mother, half crazed with grief, finally resigned herself to the thought that her little one was drowned.

Years went by. More families came and settled near the Carters. The Indians were no longer a threat, as they had retreated farther and farther into the wilderness.

The family that settled next to the Carters was very friendly. The son, a handsome youth of twenty, often came to help them in the field and do some chores for them. The Carters liked the youth and treated him as if he were their own son.

One day a hunter came to the door. "I have seen the old chief, Skenandoh," he said to Mrs. Carter. "He bade me say this to you: the ice is broken, and he knows of a hill of snow where a red berry grows. It shall be yours if you will claim it."

During the long years that she had lived in this part of the land, the woman had learned the meaning of many strange signs and words. Hardly believing what she was hearing, she asked the hunter to repeat the message. As the hunter repeated it, her face paled and she almost fainted.

The neighbor's son, who was present in the house, wanted to know the meaning of the message. The woman told him. "I must go at once," she said.

The youth glanced at the distant hills thickly

covered with woods and shook his head. "This long trip is not for you," he said. "I will go to old Skenandoh."

The sun was setting, but the youth, prompted by the urgent message, saddled his horse and set off. He sped over dark trails, and when night fell he rode on with only the stars to guide him. At dawn he came to a place called Painted Post. It had upright poles painted red. From the poles hung scalps of massacred white men. Not discouraged by the gruesome sight, he rode on among the hills that skirted Lake Seneca. Then, taking a trail leading into deep wilds, he came to a smaller lake.

The horse reared up on its hind legs as the young man pulled hard on the reins. For suddenly he came upon a wigwam near the shore. Close by was a freshly dug grave. "I must have come too late," he thought. Seeing an old Indian coming out of the wigwam, he shouted angrily, "If you are Chief Skenandoh, I came to see the red berry that grows in the snow!"

"You came in time," Skenandoh replied.

"To find this?" The youth pointed to the grave.

The chief glanced sadly at the grave, then

said, “No, it is not in that grave. My own child is buried there. Wait here.”

The chief went into his wigwam and came back leading a fair-haired girl of eighteen by the hand. She looked at the young man with wide eyes as though she had never seen a white man before.

“I named her Kayutah, the Drop Star,” the chief said. “My own child was like a sister to her. She made me promise to return the Drop Star to her mother.” Tearing the girl’s dress, he revealed her white neck and a red birthmark.

“Now,” the chief said, “I go to the setting sun.”

He filled a pouch with stones and fastened it about him. Then the old chief got into his canoe and paddled out into the lake, singing a sad Indian song. Reaching the middle of the lake, he raised his tomahawk and with one blow split the bottom of his canoe.

From the shore the Drop Star and the young man watched the canoe with the chief in it as it sank and then disappeared below the water.

“He was a good and brave man,” the Drop Star said, trying to hold back her tears.

The young man brought the girl back to her happy parents. He helped her learn the ways of the white people and eventually married her.

She took her Christian name again, but the lake where she grew up kept her Indian name. It is still known by the name of Kayutah, the Drop Star.